# Sweet Dreams, Polar Bear

**MINDY DWYER**

Alaska Northwest Books®

ANCHORAGE ■ PORTLAND

*For Sean,*
*my Alaskan dreamer*
—M. D.

Text and illustrations © 2004
by Mindy Dwyer
Published by Alaska Northwest Books®
An imprint of Graphic Arts Center
Publishing Company
P.O. Box 10306, Portland, Oregon
97296-0306
503-226-2402 / www.gacpc.com

Library of Congress Cataloging-in-Publication Data

Dwyer, Mindy, 1957-
    Sweet dreams, polar bear / text and illustrations by Mindy Dwyer.
        p. cm.
    Summary: Rhyming text imagines the fanciful dreams of animals on frigid nights in the far north,
from a shaggy musk ox going to the beauty salon to a ballet-dancing walrus.
    ISBN 0-88240-554-3 (hardbound) — ISBN 0-88240-555-1 (softbound)
    [1. Animals—Fiction. 2. Arctic regions—Fiction. 3. Dreams—Fiction. 4. Stories in rhyme.] I. Title.

PZ7.D975Sw 2004
[E]—dc22
                                                                                                2004006031

President: Charles M. Hopkins
Associate Publisher: Douglas A. Pfeiffer
Editorial Staff: Timothy W. Frew, Tricia Brown, Jean Andrews,
Kathy Howard, Jean Bond-Slaughter
Production Staff: Richard L. Owsiany, Susan Dupere
Editor: Michelle McCann
Designer: Elizabeth Watson

Jet Ski is a registered trademark of the Kawasaki Motor Company
Iditarod is a registered trademark of the Iditarod Trail Committee
Printed in Hong Kong

In the darkness of winter or summer's bright light, northern animals drift off to sleep.

Do they dream like you do? Imagine it's true.
Let's see what dream secrets they keep.

A black bear will stretch on a late summer's eve,
so drowsy from fish in her belly.

In her dreams she eats toast topped with peanutty butter
all slathered in blueberry jelly!

*Sweet dreams, sticky bear. Good night.*

Lynx love to travel through woods all night long
on the pads of their snowshoe-sized feet.

But when their eyes close, they dream of big boots
to go skiing with friends that they meet!

*Sweet dreams, racing lynx. Sleep tight.*

A little dog kicks while she sleeps on her rug, running to keep up the pace.

Of course she is dreaming, as all doggies do, of winning the Iditarod® race!

*Sweet dreams, sled doggie. Good night.*

A moose will lie down for a long night of sleep
after munching on young willow trees.

He's actually dreaming of tastier snacks—
fresh muffins and sweet herbal teas!

*Sweet dreams, munching moose. Sleep tight.*

When a musk oxen dreams, she will find some relief from the weight of her shaggy hairdo.

She envisions a trip to the local salon for a haircut and bubbly shampoo!

*Sweet dreams, bubbly ox. Good night.*

A spotted seal pup drifts into dreamland
on his nice bed of ice in the sea.

He's enjoying a dream that his spots are replaced
by zigzagging stripes and paisley!

Sweet dreams, striped seal pup. Sleep tight.

As darkness falls, lady loon makes a call,
only one haunting note for her mate.

In her dream she sings lead in a rock and roll band—
all her fans think she sounds really great!

*Sweet dreams, rockin' loon. Good night.*

A caribou's cozy on cold winter nights
after nibbling on lichen and moss.

You know that he's dreaming about plates of spaghetti
covered with dark chocolate sauce!

*Sweet dreams, caribou. Sleep tight.*

Walrus will snuggle on cool starlit nights, keeping warm in a deep walrus pile.

One dreams that she's dancing "The Nutcracker Suite" in a pink, frilly tutu. What style!

*Sweet dreams, dancing walrus. Good night.*

On bright sunny nights a salmon is snoozing
after long days of swimming upstream.

He's riding a Jet Ski®, no cares in the world,
and speeding back home in his dream!

Sweet dreams, swift salmon. Sleep tight.

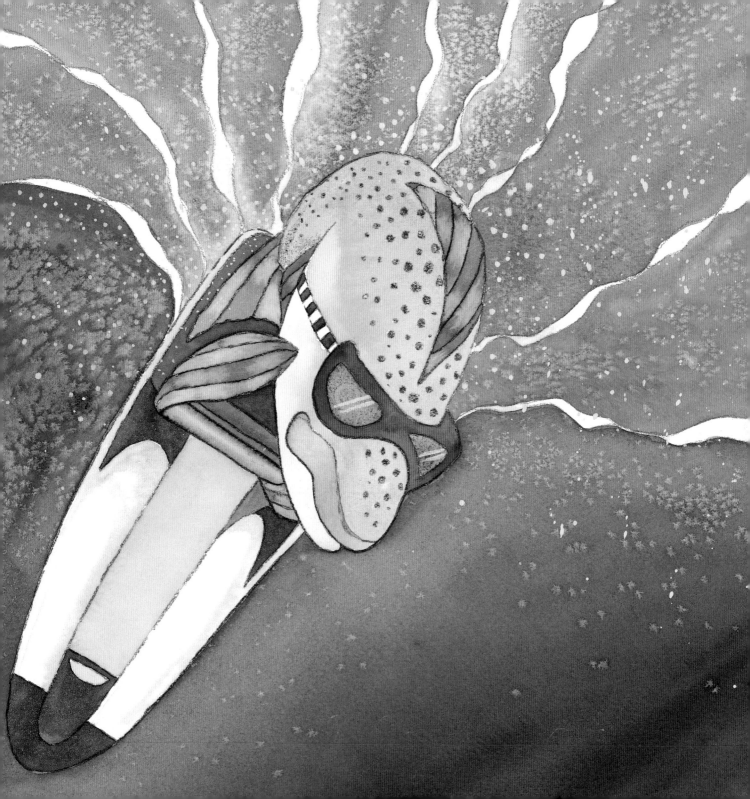

Lil' otter eats dinner by the light of the stars, cracking clams while she floats on her back.

But in dreamland she eats only chocolate chip cookies dipped in milk for a sweet bedtime snack!

*Sweet dreams, lil' otter. Good night.*

In darkness of winter, wolves sleep all day long;
while at night they sing tunes to the moon.

Asleep, they're not dreaming of all their wolf duties,
but of popcorn and goofy cartoons!

*Sweet dreams, silly wolf. Sleep tight.*

A beluga whale swims beneath waters so deep, her fair skin all shimmering white.

In her dreams she's an artist who's painting herself pretty hues of the famed northern lights!

*Sweet dreams, bright beluga. Good night.*

When a polar bear nestles right down on the ice
his fur makes him one cozy fella.

But he dreams about lying on hot, sandy beaches,
with a tropical drink and umbrella!

*Sweet dreams, polar bear. Sleep tight.*

Yes, the Northland is dreamland when day turns to night. With each sleep comes a wondrous surprise. The animals dream of incredible things, just as you will when you close your eyes.

*Sweet dreams, sleepy child. Good night.*